THE SANTA SOLUTION

If you like this book,
be sure to look for these other Apple Paperbacks
by Linda Ford:

Santa Claus, Inc.
Santa S.O.S.

THE SANTA SOLUTION

LINDA FORD

AN
APPLE
PAPERBACK

SCHOLASTIC INC.

New York Toronto London Auckland Sydney
Mexico City New Delhi Hong Kong

ISBN 0-439-21627-3

12 11 10 9 8 7 6   2 3 4 5/0

Printed in the U.S.A.   40

First Scholastic printing, November 2000

*Dedicated with love
to my nieces and nephews,
Chuck, Scott, Katie, John, Marc,
Vincent, Jonathan,
Eron, Lee Anna, Faith, Jesse,
Jennifer,
Zachariah, Elijah, and Jessicah Eva
And to the next generation,
Jessie, John,
Kayla, Ethan,
and the newest arrival, Jonathan*

THE SANTA
SOLUTION

CHAPTER

★ 1 ★

If it was up to me, I'd rather forget the Christmas that Santa Claus got sick. But I probably won't be that lucky.

It hadn't ever happened before, not *ever*. Santa *never* got sick in December. Not even a cold. I guess we thought it wasn't possible, like Santa had some kind of special insurance policy. But if he did, the policy ran out in a really big way.

Santa got the flu. And not the "I hurt all over, but I'll get by with some cough medicine" kind of flu. No. It was the "get out of my way, I've got to get to the bathroom" kind. Things were a mess.

For most people this wouldn't be a problem. A nuisance, maybe. But it was major trouble for *us* because Santa Claus is my grandfather, and it's our family business. Someday my dad will take over, and then I was supposed to do it after him. But it turns out that I'm lousy at it, and my twin sister is terrific at it. So Marcia will take over after Dad. Besides, she *wants* to.

We got the news about Granddad in the late afternoon on Christmas Eve. I'd just come home. Mom and Dad own a flower shop, and I make a tidy income delivering flowers to people. Fantastic Flowers could probably make more money by staying open later, but Dad has old-fashioned ideas.

"Christmas Eve is a time for families," he always says.

But that doesn't actually make sense, because my grandparents are never there to do the family stuff. After all, on Christmas Eve Granddad works all night and sleeps most of the next day.

It had been a long day at the flower shop. Dozens of people kept running in for last-minute gifts. I'd practically pedaled my legs off getting deliveries made. It was worth it, though. I really cleaned up on tips. Marcia and I had made a bet about who could make more money during the Christmas season. She made "designer" Christmas trees for sale.

"I win," I was able to declare when I got home and we compared earnings. Of course, she was convinced she could have made more if we hadn't been interrupted early in the season. That was when Granddad disappeared during a sleigh flight and Marcia and I went to the North Pole to help look for him. It turned out he'd fallen out of the sleigh, hit his head, and had amnesia. But it all turned out okay, except we had a week's worth of homework to catch up on.

"I lost seven whole days when I could have been getting more people interested in my Christmas trees," Marcia said.

"Ha! Mom and Dad took five orders for you while we were gone, but I couldn't make a single delivery."

"Humphfff," she sniffed.

Actually, Marcia usually isn't a bad loser. But she wasn't in a very good mood that day. I didn't find out why till later, because she had to pick up my sisters from a neighbor's house.

I was the one who took the call from Grandma on our special company phone. Then I parked myself on the stairs by the front door and waited for Dad to get home. Randolph was bringing the sleigh down from the North Pole, and Dad had to be ready to leave as soon as possible. It wasn't going to be a pretty sight. Dad is not a night person, especially after a day like Fantastic Flowers had. He'd probably have to eat the coffee straight from the jar.

"Guess what, Dad?" I announced when he appeared.

"What?" he grunted.

"Granddad's got the flu — "

"What?"

"Granddad's got the flu and needs you to take over for tonight."

He gulped and turned white. Or maybe it was green.

I didn't blame him. Of course, it wasn't as if he didn't know how to fly the sleigh. He was actually pretty good at it. Dad went through apprenticeship training years ago and takes refresher courses now and then. Plus he gets along fine with Donner, unlike me. But Dad wasn't in practice, and he didn't have time for a nap; it was going to be a rough night for him.

"Is this a joke?" Dad finally demanded.

"Dad! You know I wouldn't joke about something like that!"

"Well, I suppose not," he said rather grudgingly.

Well, that was nice! Maybe I *hadn't* wanted to be Santa Claus, but that didn't mean I didn't understand how important it was.

Dad was staring into space, kind of like a zombie.

"Dad! Dad!"

He jumped a little and looked at me.

4

"Dad, you have to get ready. Randolph's going to be here anytime now. You've got one of Granddad's spare Santa Claus suits, don't you?"

"Well, I — "

"Dad!"

"Uh . . ." He gulped. "You'd better get out of the way, Nick, I've got to get to the bathroom!"

He made it — just in time.

Mom got home twenty minutes later. She'd gone to the store for some groceries and came in with her bags loaded. I could see some eggs on top, so I didn't say anything until she'd put it all down.

"Say, Mom, we've got a problem."

"What's that, Nick?" she asked absentmindedly. She was checking a recipe card and chewing a pencil. Mom isn't a natural-born cook, and it takes all of her attention.

"I think Dad has the flu."

"That's nice," she murmured.

"Did you hear what I said?"

"Cream butter with powdered sugar and beat in two eggs before — "

"Mom! Dad's in the bathroom upstairs losing his lunch and everything else he ate this year!"

That finally caught her attention, and she looked up at me. "What's wrong with him?"

"I told you! He's got the flu."

"Oh, dear, I'd better check on him."

"But, Mom, that isn't the only problem."

"What is it?"

"Granddad's got it, too."

My mom is kind of pretty, even I can see that, but this news had her mouth opening and closing like a hungry goldfish.

"What are we going to do?" she stuttered.

I'd had a little longer to think about it and already knew the answer.

"Marcia!" I announced triumphantly.

My sister was going to be thrilled. Not about Dad or Santa getting the flu, but because she was going to have a real taste of the Christmas Eve Santa Claus business. She hadn't expected to get a chance for years and years.

I don't know why Mom was so surprised. After all, Marcia *is* in line for the Santa throne.

"She's not ready."

"She is, too."

I was right, of course. Marcia is a better pilot than Granddad, even with all his years of experience. Plus she was in practice. When Granddad disappeared after Thanksgiving, we'd flown hour after hour looking for him, only to find him in a mall playing Santa. (He thought we were nuts when we told him he really *was* Santa Claus.)

Marcia knew the equipment like clockwork; she was definitely ready.

"She's too young."

"Then we'll cancel Santa Claus this year."

"But we can't," she exclaimed, "only — " She chewed her lip and frowned.

"Randolph is going along," I reminded her.

"Oh — well, maybe if he goes, too."

Okay. So I felt a little smug. And Marcia *owed* me, although she wouldn't be thrilled about dragging Randolph along like he was her baby-sitter. Still, thanks to me she'd get to spend Christmas Eve doing what she loved best, flying that stupid sleigh.

"Why don't you go up and take care of Dad?" I suggested. "Marcia and the brats'll be home soon, and I'll help her get ready."

"Don't call them brats," Mom answered. Half the time she's on automatic pilot.

"That's a matter of opinion," I told her with dignity. Being the only boy in a mess of girls isn't my idea of *fair*.

Five minutes later Marcia and my three (three!) little sisters came home.

"Come on, Sis," I said, "we gotta talk."

"What about, what, what, what?" Sandy demanded. She's at a really obnoxious stage.

"None of your business, brat." I winked at Marcia and gave our special signal.

Being a girl, Marcia can't seem to help taking the side of the sisters part of the time, but now she sent them to the den and slipped into my bedroom. The younger girls don't know yet about Santa Claus, Inc., partly so they can have fun with Santa like everyone else for a while, and partly because they're too young to keep it a secret.

Marcia sat on my bed while I stood guard at the door to make sure Sandy wasn't trying to snoop.

"You get to be Santa Claus this year!" I announced with a flourish.

"Me?"

"Granddad has the flu, and Dad does, too."

Maybe it was too much for her to take in; there was a blank look in her eyes.

"Mom says you'll have to take Randolph, but you get to fly."

This wasn't going like I'd expected. She should have looked thrilled, but she didn't seem very happy.

"Come on, Marcia," I coaxed. "I know you're sorry about Granddad being sick, but he and Dad'll be okay, and until then you get to do it all."

"But — " She swallowed carefully, then lunged off the bed. "Get out of my way, Nicky, I've got to get to the bathroom!"

CHAPTER

2

Marcia *never* got sick. Never. But from what I overheard through the bathroom door, she was making up for it. Dad was just down the hall.

I hunted up Mom.

"We're going to have to cancel Santa Claus this year," I said firmly. "Marcia's sick, too."

"Oh . . . ," she whispered faintly.

No, Mom wasn't getting it, although having two cases of stomach flu in the house was enough to make you feel that way. But she did look like the world was crashing in around her.

My mom is generally the efficient type. She runs the house like clockwork and is probably the real genius behind Fantastic Flowers. There are also several groups, like the P.T.A., who say they couldn't get along without her. The one thing she isn't very good at is when people are sick. It's Dad who usually takes care of us, and Marcia after that. Now they were both down for the count.

Having the flu at Christmas is lousy. Especially when it cuts Santa Claus out of the picture.

"I'll wait for Randolph," I said in my most helpful voice, "and tell him he should head back north."

"But we can't cancel. . . . The children will be so disappointed and — we have a contract," she said.

Actually, we have several contracts because Santa Claus, Inc., does an awful lot of business. We have a licensing agreement with governments so people can use Santa Claus in stuff like decorations and Christmas cards and things. It wouldn't make any difference to those agreements if Santa didn't fly. But we're also in the delivery business. No, we don't make toys (and there aren't any elves), but a lot of people arrange for Santa to deliver gifts on Christmas Eve. Granddad was going to have a few problems to untangle in January.

"There isn't anything else we can do," I told her.

I didn't like the way she was suddenly examining me, kind of like a teacher just before she calls your name.

"Nicky, *you* could — "

"No, I couldn't."

"You know how to fly the sleigh and how to do everything else, and Randolph will be there to help."

"How about Randolph does it, and I stay home where I'm supposed to?"

"Does he know how?"

"Oh, I'm sure he does."

Mom just raised a skeptical eyebrow; I guess I'm not a very good liar. Of course, Randolph does know a lot about the business, but mostly from the office end. The one thing he can do is fly the sleigh as long as there's no fancy stuff, but he has never used any of the other equipment, and I doubt he's studied the routes. I had to do that when I went through apprenticeship training. Unfortunately, Mom knew about that.

"Besides, Mom," I said, trying to sound noble, "you're going to need me here to help out, what with Dad and Marcia being sick. I wouldn't feel right leaving you alone."

She didn't buy it.

"Nice try, Nick," she said. "But I can manage if I have to, and I doubt Randolph can."

I tromped down the hall to my room. My stomach felt a little upset. I hoped the flu would hit. But I was disgustingly healthy. Talk about lousy luck.

A faint knock came, and Marcia stuck a pale face around the door.

"You'll go, won't you, Nick?"

"Marcia, you've got to be crazy."

"No, but I've got the flu real bad, and it'd be awful if Santa didn't fly this year. Pleeeeease?"

My sister *knows* how much I hate that sleigh. I get airsick, and I'm more than a little nervous of heights. It's a sheer miracle that Granddad wasn't killed last month when he fell out of the stupid thing.

Marcia must have read my mind.

"Remember, Nicky," she pleaded, "Granddad installed seat belts, so you'll be perfectly safe, and you know the sleigh can't possibly crash. Even if *you* messed up, the reindeer won't let it."

That was hardly any comfort. I had a deep-down feeling that Donner wouldn't mind crashing if *I* was in the sleigh. Oh, I'm sure he doesn't want me dead, just at the South Pole.

"Besides," she continued, "you know there are antigrav cushions on the runners or else we couldn't land where there isn't any snow."

Her face was an odd shade of pale green, and her freckles stood out like they'd been dabbed there with paint.

"Ugggggh!" I groaned and tried to think. If I *did* agree to this, my own face would turn green and my stomach would feel like hers all night, at least while I was in the sleigh. Randolph wouldn't enjoy it at all. I couldn't help grinning. It would almost serve him right for the way he and the North Pole staff act around me, like I'm a cross between an ungrateful brat and a garbage-eating worm. So what if I didn't want to be Santa Claus? They really *should* get *over* it. They preferred Marcia anyhow.

"Please, Nicky?" She wasn't putting on an act; she really looked pitiful.

Sometimes it's better to just *do* a thing rather than explain for the rest of your life why you *didn't* do it. I had a sudden feeling that this was one of those times.

I sighed. "Okay."

"Thanks, Nick, you're the greatest."

Then I knew how awful she must be feeling, because usually my sister doesn't get so mushy, at least not around me.

"Just remember," I told her, "you owe me, big time."

She started to nod, then gulped and ran for the bathroom.

I'd been guilted into it, plain and simple.

Mom got Dad's spare Santa Claus suit from the closet. Of course it didn't fit, even though I put it on over my jeans and T-shirt. She didn't have time to stitch up the excess, so she used safety pins to shorten the pants and we belted in the coat. But I still looked pretty awful. A paper sack would have fit better. The cap and beard sagged like wet tissue paper. And even with my sneakers on, the boots wobbled all over my feet. We tried stuffing paper into the toes, but that put me off balance and I nearly fell on my nose.

"Oh, yeah, Mom," I told her, "I look real convincing."

"The costume is just window dressing," she answered. "And besides, you're not supposed to let people see you anyway, except maybe from a long distance. Remember, be *careful*!"

Like I didn't already know that.

I was waiting in the yard when Randolph landed. Randolph is probably the company's top executive, after Granddad, of course. He's about five feet high and built like a heavyweight wrestler. Like I said, there aren't any elves at the North Pole; it's mostly Laplanders who work there. Randolph's had it in for me ever since I tried to computerize the office and he led the entire staff out on strike.

Randolph got out of the sleigh and glanced at me, then turned back and examined me like a bug under a microscope.

"Oh, no!" he groaned.

"Yeah, it's me," I announced brightly, just to irritate him. "Dad and Marcia both have the flu, so I'm elected." I couldn't help rubbing it in. "Of course, I'll need you to come along and help me."

He looked like he was ready to quit on the spot.

CHAPTER
3

"Don't forget," Marcia said, breathing heavily as she leaned against the kitchen door, "just don't forget to give the reindeer a rest and some food every couple of hours."

"Sure, sure." I already knew that, and everything else she'd been reminding me about. It wasn't like I was a huge idiot about the Santa Claus stuff.

The team was getting their first meal of the evening. Randolph was outside with them, since Mom wouldn't let me leave until she'd made a big sack lunch to take along. Maybe Randolph would want it; I certainly wouldn't.

"You should eat some hot dinner before you

go," Mom fussed. "I'll heat up that chicken casserole."

I clutched my stomach.

"Thanks, but I'm not *that* hungry," I said.

"I thought you liked that recipe," Mom answered, a little hurt.

"It isn't the casserole, just the thought of it on the way back up."

"Oh." She screwed the lid onto the thermos of hot chocolate. "Well, maybe you *won't* get sick this time."

"Yeah, right."

"Really, Nick, maybe it's just a question of mind over matter."

"Sure, Mom. If I didn't mind, it wouldn't matter, right?"

"Now, Nick."

Marcia made her bleary way back across the kitchen floor to sit at the table. "Maybe the seat belts will help, Nick. I mean, the height won't scare you as much and maybe that's what makes you sick."

I'm sure she didn't intend to make me feel like a cowardly worm. Probably.

Mom handed me a huge sack of food, and I carried it into the backyard. Marcia stumbled out after me.

"Oh, and don't forget, Nick," Marcia said anxiously, "the toy supplier in Chicago just changed their pickup point. And remember that Blitzen has a tendency to swerve off to the left, so you've got to keep him on course."

Like the reindeer were going to do what I wanted in the first place.

"Doesn't matter," I told her, "since I'm not driving anyway."

"Randolph?" Dad's voice called from the back door.

"Gee, Dad, I think you'd better get to bed," I told him.

Randolph walked across the yard. "Yes, sir?"

"Sorry about this. But I'm sure you and Nick will do a fine job." He grinned weakly. "Maybe Nick'll even change his mind about wanting to be Santa Claus."

"Dad!" Marcia gasped.

"Sorry, punkin, just kidding."

"Ha-ha," I managed to say.

The problem was, I'm not sure he really *was* joking. Dad has no sense of humor and was too sick to tease Marcia anyway. It had only been a few months since the family had agreed Marcia could be Santa instead of me. Were they still hoping I'd change my mind?

Dad wandered back into the house. Marcia stood biting her lip. Finally she said, "Do a good job, Nick, but — "

"But not that good?"

"No. You've *got* to do a good job. Please — I just meant — oh, good luck."

She suddenly rushed inside, and I don't think it was because of her stomach. There wasn't any need to worry. Everyone had agreed she ought to be Santa. They wouldn't change their minds. I was pretty sure they wouldn't.

I felt awful.

It didn't help that the reindeer were eyeing me like they were sizing up how much damage they could do. Okay, so I'm paranoid. But they could tell I wasn't Granddad or my father or Marcia. And they didn't look any happier about flying with me than Randolph did.

"You about ready?" the Laplander grunted.

"Keep your hat on, Rudolph — uh, Randolph."

He glared like Mount Vesuvius getting ready to erupt and muttered "punk kid" before going back to remove the team's feed bags.

I'll admit, it wasn't totally an accident. I do get his name mixed up some of the time, and it makes him mad. But this time I wanted to bug him. After all, it wasn't as though I had *asked* to do this; he didn't have to act like I was the Grinch who spoiled his Christmas.

I climbed into the passenger seat and fastened the seat belt and checked *very* carefully that it was secure.

It didn't occur to me until that very moment . . . maybe I shouldn't have bugged Randolph so much, since he was in the driver's seat.

"Be careful," I warned. "Remember, I sometimes get airsick."

"Hmphfff!" he sniffed.

I might as well have kept my mouth shut.

I am *not* the noble type. If I was forced to do this Santa Claus thing, I was going to complain every chance I got. But I didn't get very many chances.

We had covered only a few towns on the East Coast when Randolph suddenly shoved the reins into my hands and hung his head over the side of the sleigh.

"I didn't know you got airsick, too," I commented when he was upright again. For the first time we had something in common. Maybe it would be the start of a whole new friendship.

"I don't," he gasped. "Can you find me a bathroom, fast?"

The flu had struck again.

A bathroom wasn't handy, but I found a deserted spot, and Randolph lurched into the darkness. I tried not to listen to his misery. Even enemies deserve their dignity.

"We'd better find you a motel," I said when he stumbled back to the sleigh.

His face was pale green, even in the moonlight.

"I can't," he gasped. "I gotta help. No way you'll handle it by yourself."

"It won't work," I argued. He stared stubbornly at me. "Look at it this way," I said, "there aren't enough airsick bags for the two of us." That thought seemed to be too much for his stomach.

"Urghhhh!"

On my honor, I hadn't said it to make him sick again. It was just the truth. I waited for him to come back.

"Okay, okay," he mumbled when he climbed into the sleigh. "Find me a motel."

I was on my own.

As in alone. Totally. If I had any sense I'd head home, or at least back to the North Pole.

But there was something about the way Randolph muttered, before heading toward the motel office, "This is a total disaster. Go home and forget the whole thing." Like I was an idiot studying to be a moron. It ticked me off.

"Says you," I muttered as I grabbed the reins and jerked my way into the air.

That did it! I'd do a great job and prove that even if I didn't *want* to be Santa Claus, I could still do a decent job. I'd be fast, efficient, and even jolly.

I just wouldn't tell anyone about it.

CHAPTER
4

To be a good Santa you need a few things.

Like . . . you gotta be able to fly a sleigh. I could do that, sort of. But it's a real challenge to hang on to the reins while you're using an airsick bag.

Another thing is that you've got to be able to use all the equipment. That was something I *could* do. My great-great-great-great-grandfather invented some terrific gadgets. Most of it must have seemed like magic back then, and even now you only read about stuff like it in science fiction. Like the Matter Energy Disassemble and Reassemble system (M*E*D*A*R). M*E*D*A*R breaks up molecules in the body (or Christmas presents) and puts them back together someplace else. It's strictly short range, pretty much from the roof to inside the house and back again. (I know, I know . . . Santa is supposed to go down the chimney. When there's one big enough and if the fire isn't burning he does. In fact, Granddad insists on it; he's a sucker for tradition. But it just isn't practical to do it everywhere.) M*E*D*A*R makes the whole Santa Claus thing possible, that and the antigrav sleigh. But using the M*E*D*A*R made me dizzy. In other words, it made me airsick. So I didn't get any relief, even when we landed.

You've also got to have a good head for keeping things organized and making sure that fifteen-year-old Buck Williamson doesn't get the baby doll that really eats and needs her diaper changed that three-year-old Becky Wilson asked for. Usually I would be fairly good at this, but it's not easy keeping things straight while your stomach is heaving and your head is swimming somewhere between New York and Chicago.

To be a good Santa Claus, you also need the cooperation of your reindeer team. Granddad and my father and Marcia don't even have to ask. I could get down on my knees and beg (not that I would; I do have *some* pride), and Donner wouldn't give me the time of day. The rest of the

24

team isn't quite as bad, but I'm still not their favorite person in the world.

Even so, I managed to cover the East Coast and start working my way west. It was weird heading back into my own town, and it was *really* weird delivering gifts to people I know.

Mr. Grainger got a Crock-Pot and *Mrs.* Grainger got a jigsaw. I was sure there'd been a mistake, but the file was definite that Mr. Grainger wanted a Crock-Pot. Lots of men cook, even my dad, but Jack Grainger was the football coach at my school.

I could hear him now. "Come on, men, don't wimp out on me, let's go in and murder the other team!"

Somehow I couldn't picture old man Grainger wearing an apron.

There was another surprise at Matt's house. He's one of my best friends, and he'd told me he asked for a basketball and season tickets to his favorite team. But the file said his top gift was a set of special paints and art paper. I didn't know he liked that stuff. Sure, Matt doodles a lot, but it's mostly cartoons of the more obnoxious teachers at school.

Actually, I thought it was kind of cool, Matt being able to paint, but I couldn't figure why he hadn't mentioned it. Maybe he thought I'd think it was geeky or something. But even if I did, I wouldn't have given him a hard time. After all, Matt stuck by me when my folks first bought Fantastic Flowers and when Stinko Jones razzed me about it every day after school.

Stinko's house came a while later. I couldn't help thinking that if this was one of those movies you sometimes see, then I'd find out what a lonely or pathetic guy he was. Wrong. Everything looked as normal as possible, although it smelled like Mrs. Jones cooked with nothing except garlic. Stinko asked for boxing gloves and a football helmet. If he'd had half a brain he would have asked for a case of mouthwash.

A while later we headed into Huntsville. Huntsville was where Granddad landed on his head last month and got amnesia. He ended up working for a week at the mall playing Santa Claus. From the notes he'd made, he remembered some of the kids extremely well.

"Acts like an obnoxious brat."

"Only knows how to scream."

"Can't get along with anyone."

"Nearly broke my knees!"

Maybe it's my imagination, but I don't think some of the Huntsville kids made a very good impression. Not that Granddad would take it out on them. Those notes were for himself, not for their gifts.

But one note said, "Sweet kid, first one I met in town."

He'd told us about Jessica Anderson and made a note to be extra careful with her delivery. Not that Santa Claus, Inc., was ever careless, but — you know what I mean. I had just finished touching up the bow on her largest package when I heard footsteps behind me.

"Who are you?" a voice asked.

Terrific, just terrific. I took a deep breath and turned around. A little girl stood there; she had dark eyes and pigtails, and she was wearing big fuzzy bunny slippers.

"Ho, ho, ho!" I laughed in the best imitation I could manage. "Don't you know who I am, Jessica? I'm Santa Claus. Ho! Ho! Ho!"

"No, you're not."

She *knew.* Somehow she knew. But maybe I could confuse her a little.

"Of course I am. Ho! Ho!"

"No, you're not," she stated again with complete confidence. "You're too short."

"Why would you say that? Ho! Ho! Ho!"

"Because I met Santa, and you're not him."

"Well, that was probably one of my helpers." I couldn't quite manage another "ho!"

"No, it wasn't."

I decided to play it straight.

"Okay, kid." I got down on my knees and looked her in the eye. "You're right, I'm not Santa Claus. He's sick, and I'm filling in for him."

Her dark eyes grew round and big. "Is he gonna be all right?"

"Oh, sure. But no one's supposed to know about it, so do me a favor and keep your mouth zipped."

She thought carefully for a minute, then nodded. "If I do, will you give him something for me?"

"Huh? Oh, sure."

She pulled a package out from under the tree and handed it over. The tag read: "To Santa, love from Jessica."

She leaned forward and whispered, "It's my dad's old football helmet."

I must have looked surprised because she added, "I saw him fall out of the sleigh and hit his head. I thought this would help next time. It's red and white." She cocked her head and looked at me. "I guess since you're helping Santa this year, you can have his milk and cookies. I made them myself."

She certainly had. They looked about as tasty as a mud pie, even if I wasn't airsick. But unlucky for me, refusing them would probably hurt her feelings.

I managed to get them down and sent the kid to bed before I activated the M*E*D*A*R and got out of there. Two minutes after I took off, the cookies went in the opposite direction. I wondered where a substitute Santa could buy more airsick bags.

At the next place, the acts-like-an-obnoxious-brat house, I unloaded the packages and piled them under a huge artificial Christmas tree. While I was bent over double-checking the tag on one of them, something whacked me across the rear end.

I turned around fast.

A six-year-old was standing there with a bat in his hand. Luckily, it was one of those lightweight hollow plastic ones or I'd have ended up in the tree. But it stung. The kid's face was red and angry.

"Ho! Ho! Ho!" I managed to get out. "That's not a very nice way to treat Santa Claus, young fellow."

"I don't care! Did you bring me what I wanted this year?" he demanded.

"Well — uh — er — I'm sure I did if your letter reached me in time."

He looked suspicious. "Don't you know?"

"Well — uh — my elves do some of the work, you see — I — uh, think they must have been the ones who took care of your presents."

"Then they don't do a very good job! Last year I wanted a train, and you brought me a crummy truck."

Now I recognized him. He was the one who started the riot at the mall.

"Sorry about that, little fellow, but I'm sure we did a better job this year."

"Don't call me *little*!" The bat swung against my knees.

"Ouch!"

He wasn't making a very good impression on me, either. He swung again, and I managed to leap five feet across a stool and behind a pile of packages. I'm not usually so athletic, but I never had so much reason before.

"Now look!" I said, then ducked again. He could move faster than me, and I ended up running a circle around the tree.

"Ouch!" He landed another one on my back-side.

Finally I activated the M*E*D*A*R to make a fast exit, but not before he caught me one last time.

I ought to have gotten hazard pay for that one. *If* they'd been paying me.

CHAPTER 5

I took my seat in the sleigh. Granddad hadn't ever mentioned something like this happening before, and I wasn't sure I should tell him. Even if I don't *want* to be Santa Claus, I don't want him to think I am an idiot who *couldn't* do it.

Towns blurred past me. I made toy pickups and deliveries. I took off, and my stomach did, too. I M*E*D*A*Red into houses and M*E*D*A*Red out. After a while my rear end stopped stinging so much, but I didn't think I'd be riding my bike for the next few days.

I was beginning to think it would be quiet for the rest of the night — until I hit the Millers' house.

Well, I didn't really *hit* it. The sleigh just sort

of banged against the chimney. But there wasn't any damage. Scout's honor.

"Whoa," I whispered to the team, and pulled them to a stop while holding my breath. The bang had been pretty loud.

"What was that?" a voice bellowed.

"Giddyap!" I hissed. But the team wouldn't budge. They knew the routine better than I did, and they knew I hadn't been inside yet.

The next thing I knew, there was a big bald man flying out the front door with a purple bathrobe on and a baseball bat in his hands. A real one this time. I guess he thought it was a burglar or something.

He held the bat over his shoulder and stared up at me. It was the first time I'd ever seen a jaw drop like they talk about in books. I couldn't move, and he just stood there with his mouth open.

"Harold?" a voice called from inside the house. "What is it, Harold?"

It broke his trance, but for a minute his jaw went up and down before he got any words out.

"Harold! Is everything all right?"

"Uh — yes, Velma."

"Then come in and shut the door; it's freezing out there."

"You've got to come and see this."

I swallowed. Not *another* witness. Granddad was going to murder me.

"Are you crazy? I'm not going out there at this time of night!"

"But, it's — uh — Santa Claus. On our roof."

"Ha-ha! Did the Easter Bunny come with him? Look, I'm going back to bed, and if you've got half a brain left you'll do the same. Don't blame me if you've got pneumonia in the morning!"

"But — it really is . . ." He shook his head and shrugged. "Oh, what's the use," he muttered. "She'll never believe it."

"Harold!"

He never even looked up again, just walked back inside. It took me a while longer to start breathing again.

I didn't dare go inside Harold and Velma's place now, so I just M*E*D*A*Red the gifts into a spot near the fireplace.

"Get going!" I ordered the reindeer. This time they moved. I'd like to think it was because I spoke with such authority that they couldn't ignore me, but I think it was because they were getting cold standing still.

It was a small town. A couple of blocks over was an old lady named Mrs. Kowalski. She was supposed to get a blender and some slippers and a new cane.

I leaned the cane up against a branch of the Christmas tree and set the other gifts beside it.

What do you know? The old lady must believe in Santa Claus; there was a glass of milk and a plate of cookies laid out with a note, "For Santa," on it. You don't usually see that unless there are children in the house.

If I hadn't been airsick, I might have been tempted. The cookies were huge and loaded with chocolate chips. Some people can't bake at all, but it looked like Mrs. Kowalski knew what she was doing in the kitchen. Maybe I should take a few along for after I was finished; I could wrap them in a napkin.

It was a mistake.

When I leaned forward to pick up the cookies, my foot nudged the cane. I grabbed for it but only managed to knock it in the other direction.

It was almost like I saw the whole thing in slow motion. The cane hit the edge of the plate. The plate slid across the table and knocked over the glass of milk. The milk hit my knee and bounced to the floor, where a big cat was sitting. The milk sloshed down my leg and filled up my boot, the cat screeched and jumped straight up my pants and onto my shoulder, then used me as a launching pad. She was headed for the chair, but the lamp got in her way, and it hit the floor next.

It happened fast. Bang! Crash! Meow! Bang! Crash! Then silence.

I must have stood frozen for five whole minutes before I heard another sound.

"Santa!" A voice screamed with joy, and a small boy launched himself at me. I managed to stay on my feet, but it wasn't easy.

"Well, young fella, how are you?" I tried to say in my deepest voice.

"I'm good, Santa, real, real good. Did ya bring me a train?"

There hadn't been any toys on the schedule for Mrs. Kowalski's house. It had to be a last-minute thing, him staying there, I mean.

"Well, I'll have to check my list. But I — didn't expect to see you here tonight. Aren't you supposed to be at your own home?"

"I asked Dad if I could stay with Grandma 'cause we don't have a chimney. Mom and Dad'll be here in the morning, but I didn't want you to forget me."

Well, that explained the milk and cookies.

"Ho! Ho! Ho! That wouldn't stop me, not for a good little boy like you."

I was sorry for the word the minute it left my mouth. Calling a kid "little" got me into trouble before. But this one didn't seem to mind.

"Okay." He yawned. Then he looked around. "Gee," he said, "you made a mess."

"Uh — sorry about that. I'll see what I can do to clean it up, but in the meantime — ho, ho, ho — you'd better get back to sleep."

"Uh-huh." He trudged upstairs.

I swept up the cookies and the broken glass from the lamp's lightbulb. There wasn't much milk on the floor, since most of it was in my boot. Then I got one of the spare gifts from the sleigh for Billy. We always carry a few, in case of emergencies. This way he'd have something in the morning before he got back home.

Before my next house, I stopped in an empty lot to clean myself up. I pulled off my boots and the red pants and tried to squeeze out some of the milk. It didn't work very well.

It was good there weren't any mirrors around, since I'd rather not see myself. The suit had taken a beating, in more ways than one, and it was pretty sad. Granddad always looked sharp in it, just like a Christmas-card Santa. He was proud of that and would probably have heart failure if he saw me now.

The sleigh started moving when I had the pants halfway back on. Drat those reindeer!

"Wait, you lousy beasts!" I yelled, then fell on my face.

It's hard to run with your pants around your knees.

CHAPTER 6

"Donner, I'm going to — " Words failed me. I couldn't think of a threat bad enough to fit the occasion.

I pulled up the red pants and tried to fasten them while running. Donner had led the sleigh into someone's yard, then stopped in the middle of a mess of Christmas decorations and stuff.

"You miserable good-for-nothing." I grabbed the harness on his head and stared him straight in the eye. "Let's get one thing straight. *I'm* Santa tonight, and you're going to do what *I* say!"

He yawned until I got a good whiff of his open mouth.

"*And* you've got bad breath!"

Grumphf. He glared.

Suddenly, I heard voices coming down the street. A whole load of people were headed my way. There was no place to hide, but the yard was really duded up with Christmas stuff, and I had most of the costume on. Maybe if we stood perfectly still.

"Quiet!" I hissed, and pulled his head. "Don't move a muscle!"

I froze into position.

Donner gave one more glare and obeyed. In other words, he shoved his nose in my face and put down his right hoof. On top of my *foot*!

There he stood, like a marble statue or something.

The boots were somewhere in the empty lot. At least I was wearing my sneakers, but that isn't enough padding under a thousand pounds of reindeer. Or at least it felt like a thousand pounds. And I couldn't even move my nose away from Donner's bad breath. What do reindeer eat to smell like that?

The group of people didn't pass by. They *stopped*. In *front* of the house.

"Yes," a woman's voice said, "this must be entry number eighty-seven."

"There's the address," another woman answered. "Oh!" She yawned. "It's getting late, but we had *so* many entries in the competition this year."

Can you believe it? Donner had landed us right in the middle of a contest. Mom and Dad entered one a couple of years ago. They spent four hundred and seventy-eight dollars and twenty-six cents getting lights and other kinds of decorations, not to mention the hours they worked on it. They were *so* proud when they got the blue ribbon and a fifty-dollar prize.

The guy who decorated this yard must have spent a fortune. Personally, I don't think grown-ups make much sense.

"The lights are very effective," a man in a blue snow jacket said. I could see a few of the judges from the corner of my eye.

"Yes, and I like the Christmas tree on the left with all the packages."

"I agree, but the rocket ship doesn't make any sense."

So that was what it was supposed to be. It didn't look much like a rocket to me, but maybe I was seeing it from the wrong angle. Besides, I think the sleigh had bent it on the way past.

"It looks like Santa and his sleigh are intended as the primary decorations."

I couldn't even swallow, just hold my breath.

We'd been on the ground long enough that I wasn't airsick anymore, but Donner's breath was making me sick to my stomach again. Not that there was anything left to come up.

"The sleigh is wonderful!"

Granddad would be pleased. It *was* a great sleigh, with neat gadgets and a top flying speed that would make most jetliners green with envy.

The group of judges walked closer. A man said, "The reindeer are splendid."

I don't know how he did it without twitching even a hair, but Donner managed to look smug at the compliment. Maybe this house would win the prize after all.

"However, I'm not impressed with their Santa Claus."

Neither was I, but that didn't help much.

"He looks so sloppy," a man complained.

"And no boots. Shouldn't Santa have big black boots?"

He certainly should, especially with a reindeer standing on his foot!

"He's too short and doesn't fit with the sleigh at all."

"And the expression on his face is hardly jolly."

"Yes — it looks more like he's in pain."

She was right about that.

"You'd think that after putting so much time

in on the sleigh they could have put at least a *little* effort into their Santa Claus."

"I'm going to mark it down as a poor presentation," a lady said.

"Too bad. If it wasn't for that Santa, they might have had a chance of winning."

I felt awful and hoped I hadn't ruined anyone's Christmas.

It seemed to take forever for them to head up the block, judge another house, then climb into their cars and drive away. I didn't dare move until they were gone.

When everything was clear, I ordered, "Off my foot, Sewer Mouth!"

I hardly saw Donner's hoof headed for me. The next thing I knew I was sitting on top of a wooden elf or dwarf or whatever it was before I landed on it.

"Ouch!" I was already tender back there, and I hoped there weren't going to be any splinters. It would be embarrassing explaining it to a doctor.

I dragged myself to my feet and rubbed my backside. Oops. The hole in my Santa pants was bigger than my hand, and the fabric hung down and flapped.

"Terrific, Donner, just terrific. What else do you have planned to make my life miserable?"

That was probably a stupid question to ask.

There was no way to turn the team around without destroying more of the decorations. I climbed into the sleigh and lifted off, then flew back to the vacant lot to collect my boots.

The first one was right where I left it, but the other seemed to be missing. I flashed the light around and found the other boot.

Or rather, I found what was left of it.

CHAPTER 7

It was a puppy. Dirty, scrawny, and miserable. But he was having a grand time chewing holes in my boot.

I could just see myself trying to explain this to Granddad.

When I took the boot away from the dog he whimpered like he'd lost his only friend. Maybe he had. He must have been abandoned.

"Sorry," I said, "but Santa Claus is supposed to have boots, right?"

"Woof."

"You're right, I'm not Santa, but no one is supposed to know."

There've been times I was sure my parents were nuts. Like when they opened a flower shop or kept having girls. Maybe it had rubbed off on me. Here I was, talking to a dog. Or maybe I was just stalling, to stay on the ground.

The puppy cocked his head and blinked. It was hard to tell what kind of dog he was underneath the dirt, but he looked sort of ugly.

The boot was even more pathetic on my foot, but I left it on anyway. Santa is *supposed* to wear black boots; I had the judges' opinion on that.

I looked at my watch and groaned. It was time to hurry into the sleigh, fasten my seat belt, and — that's when the puppy began to howl like it was dying or something.

"Aroooooooooooooooow!"

"Give me a break!" I told him.

The howling got louder. Geez! He was going to wake up the neighbors, and I'd already attracted enough attention. I unbuckled and got out of the sleigh. He stopped howling.

Maybe he was hungry. Mom had packed a huge lunch, and I wasn't planning to eat it, so the pooch might as well have some.

He practically inhaled the first sandwich before starting on the second. I climbed back into the sleigh — and he started howling again. He stopped when I got out.

"Look, dog," I told him. "I'm already doing my good deed for the night as Santa Claus."

He didn't seem impressed.

"You're dirty, and you proably smell bad, too."

He whined.

"Oh, all right! Get in!"

"Arf!"

I was right, he did smell, and he seemed to think he was supposed to sit on my lap.

"No!" I said firmly. But he obviously hadn't been to obedience training.

At the next stop I took a rope and tied the puppy onto the backseat.

"Arooooooooooooooow!"

Cripes. He wasn't very big; how did he make so much noise? I moved him into the front seat, but as long as the rope was on him, he wouldn't stop howling.

I took off the rope, and his tail started wagging.

"Okay," I said, "but remember we're on a roof, so stay in the sleigh and don't go wandering around and making noise. If you fall off, it won't be worth picking up the pieces."

I M*E*D*A*Red in and out, flew, in and out, flew, in and out. Town after town. That stupid dog wasn't the least bit afraid of flying. He stood with his hind legs on my lap and perched his front paws on the edge of the sleigh.

Things were going pretty well by the time

we reached New Mexico, and the puppy hadn't caused any major disasters. If it hadn't been for his smell, it would have been rather nice having the company.

There were a lot of lights in Albuquerque. I figured they were Christmas lights, but when I got closer I saw that they were paper bags with candles inside. Some neighborhoods must have had thousands of them. I couldn't figure out what was going on; then I remembered my apprenticeship studies in Christmas customs. Around New Mexico, and Mexico, too, I think, they light something called luminarias and let them burn all night.

Some of the houses were different, too, sort of Spanish or something. The roofs were flat, and the walls stuck up like little fences. That would make landings easier. It was nice something was going well. Then it started to rain. The suit kept me fairly dry, but the water ran down the fake hair and beard and trickled down my neck. The suit is made out of wool, and when it gets wet it starts to smell funny. It didn't help my stomach any.

Landings and takeoffs were a breeze on those flat roofs until I came to one that had those luminarias lined up all the way around on the *roof.* It scared me. What if I boggled the landing and knocked one of them over? I could barely breathe until I was down. So far, so good.

I M*E*D*A*Red in and out, only to find the puppy had left the front seat for the first time.

"Get over here!" I hissed.

He was checking out one of the luminarias and acting like he couldn't hear me.

Just as I reached him, he scooted off to the other side of the roof. Then to another. He seemed to think it was a great game, running in between the luminarias, but he was the only one of us having any fun. Finally, he stopped behind the chimney and started gnawing on a stick. I grabbed hold of him.

"Very funny," I growled.

Strange. I smelled smoke, and it seemed to be coming from right behind me. And my backside was sort of . . .

"Arf!"

"What?"

Yikes!

I dropped to my seat and rolled around fast. It didn't take long to get it out, but I lay there for a minute just to catch my breath. Overhead the stars were spinning, and suddenly Donner poked his stinky breath in my face. I pushed him out of the way.

It took a pretzel act to see what damage I'd done. I'd been careful, but I guess the torn flap from the pants had flipped into one of the candles. Good thing it was raining, after all; the wet fabric just smoldered.

"Arf?"

"Go away."

"Arf!"

He lifted a leg, and it didn't take a genius to figure out what he was planning on doing. I rolled away even faster than I had when I was on fire.

CHAPTER

★ 8

Heading west was the last thing I wanted to do. I smelled of wool and smoke and sour milk. Next time I saw Granddad, I was going to suggest arranging a place on the route for Santa to stop and take a shower. Maybe there should be a change of clothing, too. But he might not go for it.

He would probably say, "I don't usually get a boot full of milk or nearly catch on fire."

The last might be true, but who knows? Grandma once said he seemed to go through an awful lot of Santa suits. I hadn't thought much about it at the time. It was in the middle of last summer's apprenticeship training, and I'd had other things on my mind, like trying to survive.

But now I wondered what Grandma meant. I mean, if the suit fits okay and you don't have stupid accidents, then what wears it out so fast? I was definitely going to have a discussion with Grandma on the subject.

There's a lot of wide-open space between Albuquerque and California, except for a few cities like Denver and Phoenix. I managed to cover it pretty quick. The good news was that the rain stopped by the time I hit Arizona. California was more populated, and Los Angeles took plenty of time before we headed north.

I had an entire apartment building to finish on my last stop in the Bakersfield area, so I was busy for quite a while. But when I M*E*D*A*Red out, I suddenly found myself in a different world. Everything had turned white. I mean *everything*.

No. It wasn't snow, it was fog. I'd never seen anything like it. From the front seat of the sleigh I could barely see the lead reindeer. How was I supposed to fly?

In the distance a radio was playing Christmas carols. The fog muffled everything, so the music was kind of eerie. The next song was "I'm Dreaming of a White Christmas."

A snowy white Christmas would be okay, but this was a nightmare. I needed superpowered headlights, even more then red-nosed Rudolph could provide. I sat there trying to decide what to do when the sleigh started moving.

What?

"Stop, you!" I gasped, and tried to grab the reins.

While I had been trying to figure out what to do, the reindeer made their own decision. Before I could stop them, they had taken off into the solid white air.

"Whoa!"

They ignored me. No matter how hard I tugged on the reins, and no matter what I shouted at them, they just kept on going, slow but steady.

"You guys had better know where you're going!" I finally yelled.

A voice came up out of the fog.

"Hey, it's Christmas Eve. Could you hold it down?"

"Sorry," I called back.

"Say, where are you anyway? You sound like you're up a tree or something."

The voice got fainter, and I didn't bother shouting back an answer. What could I say, anyhow?

I tightened my seat belt and sank down in the seat. As thick as the fog was, there'd be no way to tell if the sleigh started to tilt, or swoop, or anything. With the antigrav it couldn't go upside down, but I wasn't taking any chances.

It was a horrible feeling, wondering if we were going to run into a tree or maybe a building. Had Granddad ever talked about foggy flights? I couldn't remember, except something he'd said about trusting your team. Sure, like I could relax, trusting a bunch of grumpy animals led by a reindeer who hates me.

There started to be some muffled sounds, like cars, and I realized we must be approaching the freeway. There was one that traveled up the center of California. Granddad said he used it for navigation. So maybe the team knew what it was doing, after all.

Jerk! Clunk!

I closed my eyes and wondered what we'd hit and how soon cars would start running over us. But it seemed like we were still moving. I sat up.

We were sitting on top of a moving truck!

"What did you idiots do?" I yelled. They ignored me, as usual.

After a couple of minutes I gathered enough nerve to look around and started breathing easier. It was a huge truck, and there was plenty of room on its flat top. And it was moving very slowly, so it was safe. All around I dimly saw other cars, all driving together. The fog was not as thick here, but maybe they wouldn't notice that the truck had a hitchhiker.

All I could do was wait for what came next. I'd rather have had something to do, because it gave me too much time to think. Dad's words kept haunting me. *Maybe Nick'll even change his mind about wanting to be Santa Claus.* So far there hadn't been any monumental disasters, not really. But that didn't mean I wanted to do it for the rest of my life.

"Would you look at that?" a voice yelled.

In the next lane was a big silver car with its windows down and a man leaning out the window. His mouth hung open. People in the cars around us were sticking their heads out and looking, too.

"I don't believe it!"

"Do you see what I see?"

I grinned weakly and called, "Where are we going?"

"Don't you know, Santa?"

"Not exactly."

"The highway patrol is taking a convoy of us through because of the fog."

"That's nice."

"Hey, are you really Santa, or is this some kind of joke?"

"It's a publicity — uuuppps." The team took off with a sudden swoosh that landed my stomach somewhere around my tonsils. A highway sign flashed by, and I could see the name of the town, so I knew which part of the gift roster I needed next. We landed on a house, the first one on the list. Donner looked at me with a terribly smug expression.

"Just luck," I growled.

"Grumphff!" He huffed back at me and let his feelings be known; I needed the pooper-scooper so I wouldn't leave his opinion of me on the roof.

It was cold and damp outside, so it was nice to M*E*D*A*R inside for a while. I didn't take long; I needed to catch up. I kept wishing there were enough time to land for a while on a deserted beach somewhere and maybe find a few shells and see what kinds of sea creatures come out in the dark. Oceanographers need to know stuff like that, and that's what I want to be.

I was depressed, and felt like yelling, "I will not be Santa Claus!"

I slapped the M*E*D*A*R button and slumped into the sleigh. The sooner I got done, the better.

"Giddyap!" I told the team.

They ignored me.

"Giddyap!!!" They acted like they were deaf.

"Come on, guys, it isn't time for your break yet, and besides, you got some rest on top of that truck you landed us on!"

If it was a fight they wanted, *I* was going to win! I got out of the sleigh and marched forward and grabbed Donner by his harness.

"I told you before, even if I didn't want to be, *I'm* in charge tonight!"

He yawned in my face, and about that time I happened to look down. I gulped. Even through the fog I could see the yard, and I was only inches from the edge. Not that it was a huge drop to the ground. It wouldn't bother me at all if I was looking out a window.

But on top of a roof is definitely not the place to argue with a reindeer.

Donner snorted. It sounded like he was laughing.

"Doggone it!"

I trudged back and got their feed bags to strap over their heads for a ten-minute snack.

"This is blackmail," I grumbled.

Okay, so I was wrong.

Donner was in charge.

CHAPTER

2

Ten minutes feels much longer when you're on top of a roof on Christmas Eve in the fog. It was cold and wet even with mittens on; my fingers felt stiff while I put everything away. And I'd always heard that California had *nice* weather!

"Get going," I growled.

At the next stop the roof was too small for landing, so we headed into the backyard. When I M*E*D*A*Red out from the house, the puppy was sniffing around a hole in the yard's hedge.

"Get back in the sleigh!" I hissed.

At that moment something knocked the puppy off his feet. He yipped, scrambled to his feet, and raced toward me, then dashed in a circle around the reindeer.

So help me, there was a kitten chasing him! A dirty, scrawny, half-grown thing less than half his size. On the second lap I grabbed for it and found the grass was really slippery.

Thunk! My face made contact with the lawn.

"Uhggh!" I spit out a mouthful of grass.

While I was lying facedown on the ground the dog scrambled onto my back and stopped. I managed to raise my head and see the cat stop, too. Then the cat turned tail and ran. The dog used my hair as a launching pad.

The cat went under the hedge. So did the puppy.

"Doggone it!" I marched to the hedge and started through the hole.

Rrrrrrippppp!

Just terrific. A branch had caught the edge of the burned fabric and — well, let's just say I was really glad I was wearing my jeans underneath the Santa pants.

In the alley the kitten was chasing the puppy again. I totally missed what *else* was in the alley.

"RRRRRUFFF!"

Gulp. I turned slowly to my left.

Now, I've seen big dogs before, but this one should have been licensed as a horse. I grabbed for the M*E*D*A*R control on my belt, but the stupid thing was missing — probably fell off when I hit the grass.

This was it. This was the end. I was dinner.

"Yip!"

The puppy was suddenly beside me, growling and challenging the other dog.

"That's nice of you, pup," I gasped, "but you might as well save yourself from turning into his appetizer. Besides, the only way you could help is if he chokes on you!"

The huge dog's lips lifted and the white teeth gleamed, even in the fog.

"Meooooooooowww! Hsssssssss!"

The kitten was back, walking stiff-legged and sort of sideways up beside the puppy. Her fur lifted till she looked about twice the size she had before, but that still wasn't as large as the big dog's *head*.

"RRRRRUFFF!"

Suddenly the cat leaped, straight at the dog's face.

"Meoooow! Hssssss!"

The kitten hung on to the dog's ears and fore-head with three sets of claws while it reached down and got the soft part of its nose with the fourth. The dog's eyes shot wide open, and it let out a howl. Rip! Slash! The dog shook its head hard, but the kitten stuck to him like glue.

Then the puppy attacked. He raced in and out, nipping with his sharp little teeth. At that moment I was glad he'd practiced his chewing on my boot.

The big dog seemed confused and suddenly let out a howl, then leaped into the air and raced down the alley. The last I saw of him, he still was getting his nose stabbed and his hind end bitten.

I might survive after all.

After a few minutes, the puppy reappeared. He strutted proudly down the alley, the cat marching shoulder to shoulder with him. Together they trotted through the hole in the hedge.

I didn't want to tear anything more off the back of my suit, so I carefully protected it on the way through the hedge.

Rrrrrriiippppp!

Well, the coat sleeve doesn't have to be completely attached, does it?

I hunted around until I found the M*E*D*A*R control, then turned to the sleigh. The kitten and the puppy sat side by side on the front seat.

"Nice try," I told the puppy, "but I'm not taking your friend along. You're enough trouble by yourself."

He whined back at me.

I gently picked up the kitten and set it on the

ground a few feet from the sleigh. The puppy scrambled after her.

"Get back in the sleigh," I told the dog.

He sat and looked at me like I was some sort of horrible person.

"I could leave you here."

He couldn't have looked more hurt if I had kicked him. I sighed.

All right, so I was feeling guilty. Of course, I wouldn't have been in the alley in the first place if they hadn't been fighting. But they did save me from getting turned into dog chow.

"All right!" I hissed, and they scrambled back into the sleigh. They looked smug, and I had a feeling I'd been taken for a sucker.

The fog started to lighten up, so we could go faster.

After we finished the West Coast and British Columbia, we headed for Hawaii. The moon was out and shone on the ocean. I couldn't resist guiding the sleigh down close above the rolling water.

I couldn't believe it. I just couldn't!

Dolphins! A pod; that's what they call a group. They saw us and shifted course to head in our direction. I slowed the sleigh to a crawl and we moved together. Then the clock on the dash of the sleigh bleeped a reminder that I was behind schedule for that longitude. I could almost hear Granddad telling me to stop fooling around and stick to my responsibilities.

But you know, I was beginning to seriously wonder if the real Santa Claus rounds were always as neat and slick as Granddad made them sound. I mean, some of the things hadn't been my fault. Granddad would still have gotten whacked on his backside by that kid. Maybe after a few glitches he slowed down to enjoy something on the way, too.

But he probably wouldn't admit it.

CHAPTER 10

Back where we live, it's cold in the winter. We get some snow, and I've shoveled my share of it. So it was pretty strange to stop in Hawaii where it was nice and warm. South America surprised me, too. I know that south of the equator, summer and winter are opposite from us, but it felt odd to find out it's really true.

It was much too warm to be wearing a Santa suit. There ought to be a way to make it air-conditioned for the hot spots, aside from the ventilation I'd accidentally ripped into my pants and coat sleeve.

With Hawaii done, it was on to Japan. That meant crossing the international date line. If we were traveling like regular people, that would have pushed us into the day after Christmas. But thanks to my genius ancestor who invented things like the antigrav, we did a time slip and slid back into Christmas.

Things would go faster now, since Santa wasn't expected in a lot of the countries I'd be hitting next. Just a stop here and there.

Japan is an awful cool country, and I wished there were more stops so I could see more. Or I did until my delivery in Okinawa.

The house didn't have a Christmas tree. I arranged the gifts near some special decorations that looked Christmassy, although not like Christmas in America. But I'd gotten pretty good at recognizing Christmas in whatever country, since Canada, Mexico, and South America have different stuff, too.

I'd just finished putting down the last gift when — whack! I jumped halfway across the room; after the last time my backside got abused I'd developed pretty good reflexes. There was a five-year-old kid yelling something at me. But I couldn't understand what he said. It was like — well, you know — a foreign language. It took a split second to hit the M*E*D*A*R button and get out of there.

I guess he didn't get what he wanted for Christmas last year, either.

In Russia, the kids expect someone named Baboushka to bring their gifts, but there was an American ambassador whose grandchildren were visiting, and *they* counted on Santa. A few stops in other countries, then to Australia. It'd be great to see some kangaroos or koalas. Well, I probably wouldn't see the kangaroos, but koalas sleep during the day, so maybe it was possible to see them at night.

Australia was hot! I know they go on picnics there instead of sleigh rides for Christmas, but this was awful. The dog and the cat wilted into a puddle on the floor of the sleigh. They glared at me like it was my fault. They roused themselves enough to follow me once to the chimney, but I M*E*D*A*Red everywhere after that.

At one of my last stops in Sydney, I hit another glitch.

Things had gone pretty well, except for the heat. (I felt like I was dying under all that padding. It was almost as bad as being airsick.) The heat did finally dry out the suit, so the wool didn't smell so bad, but it made the milk smell worse, not to mention what had rubbed off the animals onto me. I rushed through the city and came to a medium-sized house in the suburbs.

I had just put the gifts down and was checking

them off to make sure everything was included when I met Waldo.

"Howdy, mate," a voice said.

Gulp.

I whirled around and saw a man sitting in a chair, a suitcase at his feet.

"Uh — I'm not a thief," I managed to say.

"You're not Santa, either."

"I'm — uh — sort of a substitute."

"It don't bother me, just as long as I can hitch a ride with you."

"What?" I gasped.

"That's what I want for Christmas. I'm really an American, though I've lived here all my life, 'cause Mum married an Aussie. It's been nice in Australia, but it's time to leave."

Now I knew what the suitcase was for.

"I'm — uh — not sure I can do that," I told the man. "I — uh — can't pick up hitchhikers."

"Oh, I'm sure I'm a scheduled passenger. I wrote a letter months ago."

The man seemed nice and sincere and friendly; that didn't mean he could go with me. I was a little vague about international law and that sort of thing, but I was pretty sure giving him a ride would break the rules. I'd be helping him enter the country illegally, or something like that.

"Sorry," I told him. "But you'll have to catch a plane if you want to get back to the United States."

"But that's not where I want to go!"

"Then where?"

"I want to go to the North Pole and work for Santa Claus, Inc."

I ought to be used to strange things, at least I should since last year when Mom and Dad told me the truth about Santa Claus. My life has been really weird ever since. But I hadn't expected some guy in Australia to make a job application.

"Well?" he asked.

Of course, he could be a spy. I narrowed my eyes. *This was a security matter!* It took half a second to hit the M*E*D*A*R button and land on the roof. I slammed into the air and was six miles away before I stopped to radio the North Pole.

The radio works on a subatomic basis — no one can listen in. I hadn't used it so far because I didn't want anyone at the North Pole to know what I was doing. The one thing I didn't need was advice. Till now.

Grandma answered the radio call.

"Santa Claus, Inc. Nicholas, is that you?"

That's what Grandma calls my father. They

must not have told her that Dad and Marcia were sick and that I was stuck with the job.

"No, it's Nicky," I said.

"Nicky? What on earth got you up in that sleigh again?"

"Marcia and Dad have both got the flu. So I'm doing the Santa thing this year."

"Oh . . . maybe I won't tell your grandfather — not until you get home." Grandma probably thought Granddad would have a heart attack if he knew I was doing his job.

"Well, you may have to talk to him. Grandma, I've got a problem. There's this guy in Australia. He was waiting for me, and he says he wants to work for Santa Claus, Inc. I figure it's a security breach."

"Oh, my. What does Randolph say?"

"He's — uh — not with me. The flu hit him about thirty minutes out."

"Hmmmmm. You're right, Nick, I've got to talk to your grandfather about this one."

Five minutes later she was back.

"Nicky? It's all right. That was Waldingham Cunningham. He's — "

"Waldingham — Cunningham?" I asked. "You've got to be kidding."

"I thought so, too, but that's what your grandfather said. Waldingham wrote four months ago

68

and asked for a job. Security checked him out from top to bottom, and he's clear. And he's also approved for transport and employment. Your grandfather just forgot to put it down on the instructions."

Which meant I'd better head back to mend fences with Waldingham Cunningham. I really couldn't believe that was his name; what parent is sadistic enough to hang a name like that on a kid?

He was waiting.

"Waldingham?" I asked.

"Birmingham Waldingham Cunningham the third, actually." Boy, those parents were even worse than I'd thought.

"Oh. Pleased to meet you, Birmingham — uh, Waldingham — "

"It's okay, call me Waldo."

"Sure thing, Waldo."

I attached a M*E*D*A*R beacon to his sleeve, then transported us onto the roof. Waldo placed his suitcase under the front seat.

"By the way," he said, "you do know, uh — " He cleared his throat. "I mean, about your pants?"

I twisted around to look at my backside. "My goodness." I blinked at him. "I wonder how that happened?"

He took the hint and dropped the subject before climbing into the seat next to me.

"What's that?" he gulped as the kitten swiped at his leg.

"They — uh — belong with me."

"They're — charming."

He was being polite. They were dirty, scrawny, and they stank.

Suddenly, his nose wrinkled and a grimace crossed his face. I couldn't blame him. I smiled politely and said, "Sorry about that." He shrugged and didn't say anything while we picked up the next load of gifts and delivered them. "Is it always this hot?" I asked; the quiet was making me nervous.

"It's about normal for this time of year. Say, mate, how'd you end up as a Santa substitute?"

"Santa is my grandfather, and he had the flu, and so did my dad, and — "

"Oh! So you're going to be the boss man someday?"

"No, my twin sister is, but she had the flu along with everyone else."

"A girl?"

"Sure is," I told him firmly. "And she really knows how to do it, too."

"Better than you?"

"Much better."

"That's good." He looked relieved. I guess he

70

hadn't looked forward to working for an incompetent Santa.

"How long will it be until we reach the North Pole?" he asked.

The North Pole? Suddenly I felt like an idiot. All I'd been thinking about was getting back to my own house. But I couldn't head straight back home after this nightmare was finished. No. The team and the sleigh had to be returned north, and Randolph wasn't there anymore to do it. Of course, the reindeer could probably get home on their own, but I couldn't trust Donner not to do something rotten on the way. Besides, now there was Waldo. Even if security had cleared him, I wasn't about to turn Santa's sleigh over to a perfect stranger.

The next few stops were routine, which was good, because I was too depressed to think straight. I love my grandparents, but I'd been hoping to avoid Granddad until Christmas had started to blur a little in everyone's memory. As it was, I was going to have to stash the suit in a safe hiding place until I could dump it. There was no way it could be saved.

When we stopped at the next house, Waldo climbed out. "I think I'll get some air," he explained. "The animals — you know."

"Just don't make any noise."

"Like a mouse."

His idea of a mouse would make a kangaroo sound quiet. I hurried so I could get back up there before he woke everyone up. I M*E*D*A*Red up and tiptoed to his side.

"You've got to be more quiet!" I hissed.

"Sorry," he answered. His nose wrinkled, and he leaned over to sniff at me.

"Oh," he said, "it's you — never mind. Say, mate, do you mind if I sit in the backseat?"

I could hardly blame him. I'd rather move a couple of seats away from me, too.

CHAPTER 11

After Africa, there was just Europe and Greenland left. By the time we reached the North Pole, it was about two on Christmas morning. I'd left my own house around eleven Christmas Eve, but thanks to the time slip, we got back only three or four hours after we left — to everyone else, of course. For me it was closer to twenty hours; it felt like twenty years.

"You're late," was all one of the stable hands said when I landed.

"Poor boy." No, he wasn't talking to me. It was Donner that got all the attention.

"This is Birmingham Waldingham Cunningham," I told one of the reindeer wranglers. "He's come to work for Santa Claus, Inc. Could you find him an apartment and show him where to go?"

"Think you're the boss, do you?" he grumbled, but he did lead Waldo in the direction of the underground staff quarters.

"And could someone take me home after I see Grandma?" I asked.

"Glad to!" one man said. He didn't have to sound so happy to get rid of me.

The puppy and the kitten were fast asleep.

I climbed from the sleigh and heard snorts of laughter as they saw my backside. I'd given up the idea of hiding the suit; Waldo would tell them about it. And if I had to show myself anyway, I was going to get a shower before heading home. Besides, I was caught between two things. If Granddad knew everything, I'd be in for it, but on the other side, it might convince everyone that I was the absolute *last* person to be Santa. Thinking about it gave me a headache.

"Nicky!" Grandma exclaimed, "you're — " Her nose wrinkled.

"Don't worry," I told her, "I'm heading for the shower. Can I borrow some old clothes?"

"I'll put them out for you."

I was really glad to get clean. The suit disappeared while I was in the shower.

"You want something to eat?" Grandma asked when I came out, wearing some cinched-in clothing of Granddad's.

"You've got to be kidding! I still gotta fly home."

"That's right. Sorry."

"Granddad isn't awake — uh — is he?" I had a feeling that if he was awake I was somehow obligated to go say Merry Christmas, and who knew what might happen after that?"

Her eyes twinkled. "He was a little while ago, but if you slip out very quickly — "

"Thanks." I gave her a quick hug. "Merry Christmas."

I was halfway to the stable before I remembered I hadn't asked her about the disasterized Santa Claus suit. Well, I'd have to trust that she'd deal with the evidence.

Dad and Marcia weren't much better when I got back. But Mom was upset. She hadn't remembered until after I left that the flight wasn't just a few hours but nearly a day long for the one flying the sleigh. It's easy to do that — the time slip is kind of confusing. I guess Mom wouldn't have asked me to go if she'd remembered that part. So she'd spent the whole time worrying.

"Why didn't you call?" she demanded.

I reminded her, "You know we can't relay from the sleigh to the house."

"Well, you could have found a telephone."

"I didn't have any time!"

Before I went to bed, I stuck the animals in the garage. The puppy whined and looked mortally wounded.

"It's warm and dry," I told him, "and a lot cleaner than you are."

I planned to stay in bed till New Year's Day, but Mom knocked on my door at ten the next morning.

"Leave me alone," I mumbled.

"Nick, I'm sorry to get you up, but you've got to do something about that smelly beast you brought home. He started howling two hours ago and hasn't stopped. The neighbors are complaining."

I dragged myself downstairs and gave the puppy a bath. He wasn't quite as ugly when he was clean. The kitten sat on the shelf above the tub and washed herself at the same time. The night before I'd thought she was mostly black, but she turned out to have dark tiger stripes.

When the puppy was dry he and the cat followed me into the house. Mom didn't like it, but she just rolled her eyes while I stopped in the kitchen to eat three or four sandwiches.

Then the three of us crawled into bed and slept till the next morning. Marcia and Dad were over the flu by then, and Dad had plenty of questions.

"You had a great time, didn't you?" he said heartily. "Of course, we thought Randolph was with you, but I suppose it was a fine adventure all the same. Maybe you've just needed time to grow into the job."

Marcia looked like the world had fallen down.

"I still don't want to be Santa," I said quickly.

"You really should reconsider, Nick," Dad told me. "It's your heritage."

"It's Marcia's heritage, too, and she can have my share."

"But it's a great job, isn't it?"

"Sure, Dad, as long as your life insurance is paid up."

CHAPTER 12

Dad didn't notice the headlines until the next evening. And then he sent the little sisters upstairs to watch television so the rest of us could have a "discussion."

MAN SEES SANTA ON ROOF.

KID SAYS HE RAN SANTA OFF THE BLOCK.

SANTA HITCHES A RIDE.

MAN SAYS SANTA CLAUS RUINED CHRISTMAS CONTEST.

There were more, except that some were cutesy holiday pieces that weren't connected to my activities. But the others told a few details I'd have rather kept to myself.

"What on earth did you do that night?" Dad demanded.

"So I ran into a few glitches," I defended myself. "I told you I wasn't cut out to be Santa."

He looked awfully disappointed. Then he turned suspicious.

"Did you mess up just to get out of being Santa Claus?"

"Of course he didn't," Marcia said before I could say a word. "He'd never make a mess of it on *purpose*, would you, Nick?"

I'm not sure whether she was defending me or saying I was a clumsy moron. Or maybe a little of both.

I ignored it and settled back to eat some more cookies. After that sleigh ride I had to catch up on my eating.

"But I *would* like to hear all the details," Marcia said. "Come on, Nick, now that you've caught up on sleep and if you can stop feeding your face for a minute, tell us what it was like, or — maybe later." She winked. I guess she figured I'd be more honest if she was the only one listening.

The doorbell rang, and Mom went to answer it.

"Guess who's here?" Mom asked from the doorway.

"The tooth fairy," I answered grumpily.

"It's Santa Claus."

Oh, no. It was Granddad.

"Dad," my father exclaimed, "what are you doing here *now*?"

My grandparents live just down the street, but they're at the North Pole a lot and *always* there from November through mid-January. It would take a major disaster to drag Granddad away two days after Christmas. A major disaster, like his grandson making a mess of Santa Claus? He had a bunch of newspaper clippings in his hand. This wasn't going to be pretty.

I sank deeper in the couch and tried to be invisible. It didn't work.

"I'm here to have a talk with Nick," he said. "Alone."

Maybe he didn't want witnesses when he murdered me.

"Glad you're over the flu," I told him quickly. "If you were as sick as Marcia and Dad, well, you must have been pretty miserable."

"Oh, yes, uh, thanks." He seemed distracted, like he didn't know what to say. That was a surprise. I'd have thought he rehearsed the lecture all the way south.

"You *are* feeling better, aren't you?"

"Yes. Uh — so — " He glanced at the newspaper headlines. "Are all of these about you?"

"Not *all* of them."

"But a lot of them, right?"

I nodded. Might as well get it over with. "Sorry, Granddad, but I did the best I could."

"Hmmmm. I saw your Santa suit when you walked in, and I, uh, caught a whiff when you walked down the hallway."

I winced at the memory.

"Uh, Nick. Have you told your father or Marcia about — everything?"

"Not yet. Why?"

"How about keeping it our little secret?"

My jaw nearly hit the floor. "What?"

"Uh, you've probably guessed that things don't always go as smoothly as they could."

I had figured that but didn't think he'd ever admit it. "Yeah."

"Weeeellll, let's not bother anyone else with the details. We could just let them find out on their own." Suddenly he winked. "We'll let them wait until they're old enough to handle reality."

I guess Granddad has a sense of humor after all.

He didn't stay after that, just said he had a lot of work to catch up on since being sick.

"Was Granddad really mad?" Marcia asked. "I mean, was it awful?"

"Grueling," I told her, and tried to look devastated. "He gave me the third degree and a lecture. But the good news is that I don't think he minds you being Santa Claus anymore."

Marcia brightened. "Really? I mean, well, I'm sorry it was hard for you, but — you know."

"No problem." I shrugged as though I was upset but putting on a brave front for her sake.

"So tell me about being Santa."

"That? Oh, you'll find out."

"Come on, Nick."

She kept bugging me, but that's all I would say, since I'd promised Granddad.

"Gee," she finally said, "I think that's mean. I'm going to have to wait for years and years before I get to be Santa."

Maybe Marcia won't mind reality that much when she gets to it. After all, Granddad's been doing it for years now, and he doesn't want to retire. Mostly he even seems to enjoy his job.

But for myself, I'd rather have the flu.

'Tis the Season to Be Reading!

All titles: $4.50 US

Available wherever you buy books, or use this order form.